PETE'S A PIZZA

WILLIAM STEIG

SCHOLASTIC INC.

New York Toronto London Auckland Sydney
Mexico City New Delhi Hong Kong

PETE'S IN A BAD MOOD. JUST WHEN HE'S SUPPOSED

TO PLAY BALL WITH THE GUYS, IT DECIDES TO RAIN.

PETE'S FATHER CAN'T HELP NOTICING

HOW MISERABLE HIS SON IS.

HE THINKS IT MIGHT CHEER PETE UP

TO BE MADE INTO A PIZZA.

SO HE SETS HIM DOWN ON THE KITCHEN TABLE

AND STARTS KNEADING THE DOUGH

AND STRETCHING IT

THIS WAY AND THAT.

NOW THE DOUGH GETS WHIRLED

AND TWIRLED UP IN THE AIR.

NEXT, SOME OIL IS GENEROUSLY APPLIED.

(IT'S REALLY WATER.)

THEN COMES SOME FLOUR.

(IT'S REALLY TALCUM POWDER.)

AND THEN SOME TOMATOES.

(THEY'RE REALLY CHECKERS.)

PETE CAN'T HELP GIGGLING WHEN HIS MOTHER SAYS
SHE DOESN'T LIKE TOMATOES ON HER PIZZA.

"ALL RIGHT," SAYS HIS FATHER, "NO TOMATOES, JUST SOME CHEESE." (THE CHEESE IS PIECES OF PAPER.)

"HOW ABOUT SOME PEPPERONI, PETEY?"

PETE CAN'T ANSWER BECAUSE HE'S ONLY

SOME DOUGH AND STUFF.

BUT WHEN THAT DOUGH GETS TICKLED,

IT LAUGHS LIKE CRAZY.

"PIZZAS ARE NOT SUPPOSED TO LAUGH!"

"PIZZA-MAKERS ARE NOT SUPPOSED

TO TICKLE THEIR PIZZAS!"

"WELL," SAYS HIS FATHER, "IT'S TIME FOR THIS PIZZA TO BE PUT IN THE OVEN."

"AH! NOW OUR PIZZA IS NICE AND HOT!"

PETE'S FATHER BRINGS THE PIZZA TO THE TABLE.

"IT'S TIME TO SLICE OUR PIZZA," HE SAYS.

BUT THE PIZZA RUNS AWAY AND

THE PIZZA-MAKER CHASES HIM.

THE PIZZA GETS CAPTURED AND HUGGED.

NOW THE SUN HAS COME OUT.

AND SO THE PIZZA DECIDES TO GO

LOOK FOR HIS FRIENDS.

FOR MAGGIE,

MY ORIGINAL PIZZA

ISBN 0-439-10475-0

Copyright © 1998 William Steig.
All rights reserved.
Published by Scholastic Inc., 555 Broadway, New York, NY 10012,
by arrangement with HarperCollins Publishers.
SCHOLASTIC and associated logos are trademarks and/or registered trademarks
of Scholastic Inc.

12 11 10 9 8 7 6 5 4 3 2 1   9/9 0 1 2 3 4/0

Printed in the U.S.A.   08

First Scholastic printing, September 1999

Designed by Cynthia Krupat